To Lee-Anne with lots of Love
& Kisses on your
5th Birthday
from

Granny

xxxxxxx

101
Two-Minute
Tales

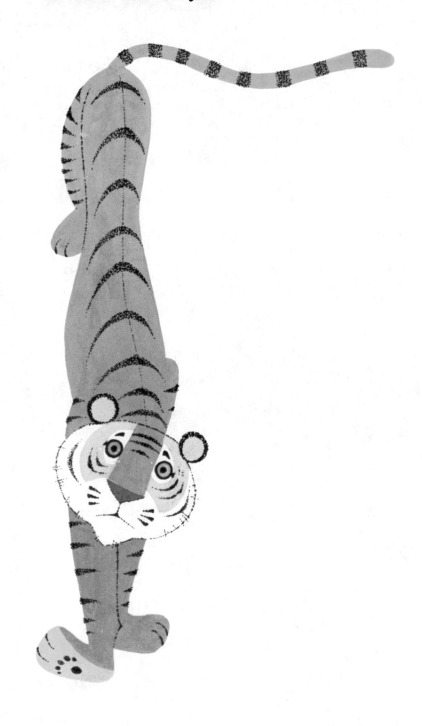

101
TWO-MINUTE
TALES

TREASURE PRESS

First published in Great Britain in 1982 by
Cathay Books

This edition published in 1986 by
Treasure Press
59 Grosvenor Street
London W1

Copyright © 1982 Martspress Limited
This edition copyright © 1982 Cathay Books

Reprinted 1987

ISBN 1 85051 108 X

Printed in Hong Kong

Contents

Blackbird, blackbird

"Blackbird, blackbird, on the fence,
"How many pence in twenty pence?"
"Four times four and then four more!"
"Smartest bird I ever saw!"

"Blackbird, blackbird, please do tell,
"Who pushed pussy down the well?"
"It was bad boy Tommy Green!
"Naughtiest lad I've ever seen!"

Two for tea

"Have another banana, Mickey Monkey, and tell me what elephants have that no other animals have," said Edward Elephant.

"That's easy," replied Mickey. "Little elephants, of course. What did the baby porcupine say when he backed into a cactus?"

"He said 'Is that you, Ma?'" chuckled Edward. "I say, does Georgie Giraffe get a sore throat if he gets his feet wet?"

"Of course he does, but not until next week," answered Mickey. "Time I went home."

"Leave the grapes behind," grunted Edward.

Three little pigs

Once upon a time there were three little pigs who thought they knew *everything*. Real little know-alls they were. One day they decided that they were far too clever to go on living any longer with their silly old mother, and they set off down the lane, leaving their comfy pig-sty behind them.

They hadn't trotted very far when, rounding a bend, they came face to face with a Big Bad Wolf. Now, the three little pigs had never seen a Big Bad Wolf before, so they all gave the wolf a friendly smile.

"We three have left home because we're too clever to live with our silly mother," said Porky, the eldest.

"Is that so?" grinned the wolf. 'Well, since you're so clever, perhaps you can tell me what I'm having for supper tonight?"

Of course, the little pigs didn't know.

"*Pork sausages!*" growled the wolf, baring his teeth and licking his lips with his pink tongue.

"Porky," whispered Percy, the youngest little pig. "Something tells me we're not so clever after all. I want to go home."

"So do I," murmured Porky. "So, brothers, let's go home." Too late! The wolf was about to pounce. Suddenly, behind the Big Bad Wolf there was a great grunt. He leapt in terror and was off like the wind.

"Mummy's not so silly, is she?" said Porky, pleased to be safe, again.

Bold Sir Basil

Have you ever heard the story of bold Sir Basil Bottle who saved the lovely Princess Gloria from the clutches of a wicked dragon? You haven't? Well, that's not surprising, because it has never been told before so you're very lucky to hear it now.

It seems that a wicked dragon, whose nam was Douglas, had laid siege to the castle where the beautiful Princess Gloria lived, and he stoutly refused to go away until the princess married him. The princess was aghast.

"Marry a dragon?" she cried. "Impossible! I shall, however, marry the man who can rid me of this upstart dragon!"

Then brave knights came from far and near to do battle with Douglas the Dragon. But the great beast drove them off, one after another. Then one day, there came a certain handsome young knight named Sir Basil Bottle of Banstead, renowned throughout the land for his sharp wits and empty pockets.

There he stood boldly, outside the castle, drawn sword in hand. Suddenly he threw it from him. He shouted a few words to the dragon. The enormous monster nodded its ugly head, blew a gust of flame or two, and lumbered off, never to be seen by the princess or anyone else again.

"All dragons," explained Sir Basil to the princess, "love black puddings and cream buns. I promised you'd send a cartload every day if he would go away. It was an offer he couldn't refuse." And so Sir Basil won the hand of the princess.

The red ball

Jilly was still chuckling to herself. She had just come home with her mummy after a visit to the electrician's shop.

"Why didn't you call and repair my doorbell yesterday, as you promised?" her mother had said to the electrician.

"I *did* call," replied the electrician, "but you must have been out, because I rang three times and there was no reply." And little Jilly laughed and laughed.

Now she was playing in the garden with her favourite red ball. In the garden next door was Jilly's best friend, Tommy Brown. When he saw Jilly throwing the ball up into the air and catching it, he called to her.

"I say, Jilly, why was Cinderella stopped from playing netball?"

"Goodness, how should I know?" said Jilly.

"Because she ran away from the ball, of course." And Tommy laughed and laughed.

"So she did! Now why didn't I think of that," said Jilly. "You *are* funny, Tommy."

Sausage jokes

Here is Bob the butcher with Bill, his faithful bulldog. Bob is always telling jokes about sausages, and his customers know that if they don't laugh, Bill might bite them. He never does, because Bob's jokes *always* make people laugh.

For instance: "A man in a restaurant asked. 'May I have some sausages, please?' To which the waiter replied. 'With pleasure.'

'No,' said the man, 'with pickles and chips.' Later he called. 'Waiter, I can't eat these sausages. Call the manager.'

But the waiter replied 'It's no use, sir. He can't eat them either.' "

Then again: "What did the fat man say when he sat down to eat a big plateful of sausages? 'I'm afraid these sausages are all going to waist.' "

And here's another of Bob's sausage jokes: "An angry customer took back some sausages she had bought from her butcher. 'These are all meat at one end and sawdust at the other,' she shouted.

'Yes, ma'am,' said the butcher. 'In these hard times it's difficult to make both ends meat, is it not?' "

Did *you* laugh at Bob's sausage jokes?

Brian Brownbear

Mrs. Brownbear was cooking breakfast for her little son Brian.

"What a funny little chap he is," she was thinking. "This morning he asked me how I found out he hadn't taken a bath. 'You forgot to wet the soap,' " she had told him.

Next day Brian ran in to tell his mother he had found a horseshoe. "Do you know what that means?" She asked him. And he said, "Yes, Mummy, it means that some poor horse is running around in its stocking feet." Then he told her he wasn't going to school any more. "Why not?" she asked. "Well," he said. "On Monday teacher said five and five make ten. On Tuesday she told us six and four make ten. Yesterday she said seven and three make ten. So I'm not going back to school again until she makes up her mind."

Mrs. Brownbear was still laughing when she heard a crash from the dining room.

"What was that, Brian?" she called out.

"You know that plate you're always worrying I will break?" came Brian's voice. "Well, your worries are over!"

"Huh! He's not so funny after all," grumbled Mrs. Brownbear.

9

The weary knight

When good King Arthur ruled the land, there were many brave knights who fought for the honour of England. It happened one stormy night that a knight of King Arthur charged into an inn.

"Quick, oaf – lend me a horse," he shouted rudely to the inn-keeper. "My own steed is too weary to go another step and I must reach King Arthur's castle this night."

"Sir Knight," replied the inn-keeper politely, listening to the raging of the storm outside. "I have no horse to lend you. The only animal I have is that big old shaggy dog by the fire."

"Very well," said the bad-tempered knight. "I shall ride him."

"Oh no, your lordship," cried the inn-keeper. "I wouldn't send a knight out on a dog like this," and he laughed.

"Hmm! You're very obviously a very clever chap," snapped the knight. "So tell me – why couldn't King Arthur find his page?"

"Because he had closed his book," chuckled the inn-keeper who *was* a clever chap. As for the weary knight, he went out into the night.

Smart Alec

"Come along, Alec," said Alec's mummy. "It's time to get up and get dressed. How do you find yourself this morning?"

"Same as usual, Mummy," grinned Alec. "I just open my eyes and here I am."

"Oh, so you're being smart again, are you?" smiled his mummy . "I'll put the question another way then. How did you sleep last night?"

"On my back with my eyes closed," replied Alec cheekily.

"Really, Alec," said his mummy. "I meant did you sleep well – or not?"

"No, not very well," answered Alec.

"Why not?"

"Well, you see, I kept having the same dream. It was about a door with a sign on it. I pushed and pushed but I just couldn't open the door."

"What was on the sign?" asked his mummy.

"*Pull!*" laughed Alec merrily.

"I'll tweak your ears if you don't jump out of bed and get dressed at once," his mummy told him. "It's almost time for school. Tell me, how do you like school?"

"Closed!" snorted Alec, running downstairs as fast as he could.

The grubby teddy

Linda had a brown Teddy Bear. She loved him very much and called him Brownie. He had belonged to her mummy when she was little. One day Linda said to Brownie: "You *do* look grubby! I will give you a good wash tomorrow as soon as I get up."

Brownie didn't like that idea at all. He had *never* been washed. "If only I could move like *you*," he said to Pippa, the black cat, when they were alone. "I would hide."

Pippa wanted to help Brownie. So she dragged him outside, up the muddy path and hid him behind a bush. He was even dirtier then than he had been before.

Next day the postman found Teddy when he came with the letters. Linda took him upstairs to the bathroom with her that evening. She put him into her warm sudsy bath and *scrubbed* him. Soon the mud, dirt and dust fell from Brownie and then – what a surprise! Brownie wasn't really brown at all – underneath he was strawberry pink! Mummy who had owned him so many years ago had forgotten that. He quickly dried in front of the fire and they all had supper together – Linda, Pippa and Brownie, who after that day was called Pinky!

Herbert's tail

It was market day and Herbert Hare had overslept. He hurriedly dressed, cleaned his teeth and ran down the road. The best lettuces would be sold if he didn't get there quickly.

On the way he met Rona Rabbit. "Hello, Herbert!" she called. "How did you lose your tail?" Herbert couldn't believe his ears. He looked round and sure enough, Rona was right. His tail was no longer there! He was sure his tail had been there yesterday, and all the way along the road and back again he looked *everywhere* for it.

He forgot all about the lettuces and went home. The tail wasn't at home either. At last Herbert decided to undress. When he took his trousers off, there was his tail, still attached to him, in the right place! He had dressed so quickly that morning that he had put his trousers on back to front! He *was* pleased to find his tail again.

Hoppy learns to hop

Hoppy was a happy frog. Happy Hoppy his friends called him. Mind you, no one could ever understand why, because although Happy Hoppy was happy, he wasn't much good at hopping. He could never seem to get the knack somehow. Well, hopping took so much effort. Walking was much easier.

But then one day Happy Hoppy met Puppy Poppy. Puppy Poppy was very snappy and yappy. She also liked chasing frogs. So snappy, yappy, Puppy Poppy chased Happy Hoppy, and the snappy yapping startled Happy Hoppy so much that he almost jumped out of his skin. In fact he *hopped*. And he found he liked it.

The big ships

In the days before engines were invented big ships roared through the rolling waves with nothing but the wind in their sails to help them along.

And roar they certainly did. When every sail was set on a tall ship and the wild wind strained against the canvas and ripped along the ropes and bent the masts, the ships would sound like live animals struggling over the water and screaming and groaning as they went.

The sea creatures were very puzzled by these huge monsters which always swam on top of the sea and never seemed to stop to eat anything at all.

The whales didn't like them at all. They thought they were a new kind of whale. Sometimes the whales even charged at the ships and attacked them.

"Well, I won't stop trying," said one whale after making an attack, "but these new creatures certainly have tough skins."

The speeding trains

Tommy was a lucky boy. He had a marvellous train set. The tracks were set up on a table which looked like a country village complete with duck pond, bridge, trees and roads.

All the engines and carriages were in perfect working order and always whizzed round just as they were supposed to. They never broke down or jumped off the tracks.

There was only one thing wrong with having such a marvellous train set.

Tommy was never invited out to tea.

All Tommy's friends always wanted to come to tea with *him* so that they could play with his train set.

"We will send round some cakes and sausage rolls," his friends' mothers would say, "just as long as the children can come and play with the train set. They do love it so."

Poor little Tommy! He loved his train set too, but sometimes he did feel like going out and playing with someone else's toys, just for a change.

But then Tommy had a stroke of luck. A boy moved in up the road who had an electric car racing track. Suddenly everyone became mad on car racing.

So then, everyone, including Tommy, went to tea at the new boy's house. How Tommy did enjoy the change, especially as the new boy's mother made scrumptious egg and tomato sandwiches.

And after that, Tommy and the new boy took turns at going to tea at each other's houses, which was great fun for both of them.

The rabbits

Once upon a time there was a family of rabbits who lived in the country.

At least they thought they were rabbits. Everyone had always said they were rabbits. But then one day they were playing in a field when Flopsy Rabbit heard a little girl say: "Look at those sweet bunnies!"

"Are we rabbits or are we bunnies?" Flopsy asked her brother, Chomper.

And then just to confuse things even more, they heard the girl's mother say: "Yes, bunny rabbits are little ducks, aren't they?"

"Yes," said the little girl.

"Well, are we rabbits or are we bunnies or are we bunny rabbits or are we little ducks?" continued Flopsy. "Because if we are little ducks, we should go down and start swimming in the duck pond and I don't fancy *that* much."

It was all very confusing.

Then one of the other rabbits called Fluff scratched her ear.

"Well, I don't *know* if I'm a bunny or a rabbit or a little duck or a bunny rabbit, but there is one thing I'm *sure* I am."

"What's that?" asked Chomper.

"Hungry," grinned Fluff. "Let's all go home for tea."

And they did.

They had a lovely tea of grass and dandelion sandwiches.

Colin Clown

Tootle-toot-toot! Colin Clown blew on his trumpet. He wanted everyone to listen to his funny jokes.

"If one man is carrying two sacks of grain and another is carrying three sacks, which man is carrying the heavier load?" asked Colin with a smile on his face.

"Why, the man with three sacks of course," everyone answered.

"No," grinned Colin. "The *three* sacks hadn't anything in them – ho, ho!"

"Now, here's a question for you, Colin," a voice called. "What time is it when a clock strikes thirteen?"

"There's no such time," scoffed Colin, who was good at asking questions but not at answering them.

"When a clock strikes thirteen, it's *time* to get it *mended*," laughed the voice.

Colin felt huffy, because after all, *clowns* are supposed to make the jokes. "How old are you?" he asked.

"Fifteen," replied the voice.

"Well, if you want to be sixteen, leave the jokes to me," warned Colin.

Pussy Cat

Pussy Cat, Pussy Cat, where have you been?
I've been to London to see the queen.
Pussy Cat, Pussy Cat, what did you there?
Well, the queen was out, so I saw the mayor.

Pussy Cat, Pussy Cat, what did he say?
He said politely: To you, good-day!
Pussy Cat, Pussy Cat, saw you his house?
Oh yes indeed – and in it a mouse!

Pussy Cat, Pussy Cat, then what said he?
He said: You can have that mouse for tea!
Pussy Cat, Pussy Cat, what did you say?
I said: Not me – I'm on holiday!"

Pussy Cat, Pussy Cat, did he say more?
No, not a word – he showed me the door.
Pussy Cat, Pussy Cat, what did you then?
I caught a train and came home again.

15

Claire's new pram

One morning Claire opened her eyes and found a beautiful new doll's pram at the side of her bed.

Clare had never seen the pram before and she hadn't heard anyone bring it into her room.

But the strange thing was, Clair wasn't in the least surprised to see the pram standing there.

Most people would have been amazed to wake up and see a strange doll's pram standing at the side of their bed, but Claire was not at all surprised.

Claire just woke up Dolly from her cot and put her in the pram and took her for a walk along to Mummy's and Daddy's room. Because, as you have probably guessed, this was Claire's *birthday* and she knew that the doll's pram must be a birthday present!

A spring feast

The winter snow melted and the spring sun shone and Red Squirrel, who had dozed through the long cold months, scurried round looking for food.

But there wasn't much for him to find, because nuts, which Red Squirrel liked, didn't ripen till the autumn.

Luckily Red Squirrel knew a garden, where some children always put out peanuts for him. So he hurried along there and had a real feast. "Thank goodness for children," he thought.

The magic car

Once there was a magic car that liked to ask riddles.

"What sort of pets do cars like best?" asked the magic car.

"*Car*pets of course," smiled Timmy, who was riding in the car.

"All right then, why isn't the sun heavy?" asked the car.

"Because it is so light," laughed Timmy.

"Now, here is a very difficult question," said the car, "how many sides has a sausage?"

"Sausages are round. They have no sides" said Timmy.

"Oh yes, they do," laughed the car, "they have two sides – an inside and an outside."

"That reminds me," cried Timmy, "it's time to go home. We are having sausages for tea."

Penniless pigs

"What is worse than running out of pennies?" asked Prunella Pig.

"Why, running out of pound notes, of course," gasped Percival Pig.

"Don't be silly" laughed Prunella. "If you run out of pennies or out of pounds, it's the same – you have run out of money. No, worse than running out of pennies is running out of the house without a coat and finding it's raining!"

The runaway

Naughty Norman one fine day,
Thought that he would run away.
He left his desk and crossed the floor
And ran out through the open door.
He threw his books upon the ground,
To make a wumpy, thumpy sound.
He said: "I'm going off to play.
I'll come to school another day."
Little did young Norman know,
Teacher was glad to see him go.

17

Farmer Dick

There was an old farmer named Dick
Who tickled his bull with a stick.
The bull with a bellow,
Said "You're a quaint fellow,"
And gave Farmer Dick a quick kick.

That jolly old farmer named Dick
Then played on the bull a sly trick.
He tied an old pail
To the bull's shaggy tail,
The bull growled, "Now that's a bit thick."

In fury, it then kicked a brick
Which damaged the nose of old Dick
Said the farmer "Okay!
"Let's call it a day!"
And clouted the bull with a pick.

Its lips then the bullock did lick
And smilingly said "Not so quick!"
It trod on Dick's corns
Then lowered its horns
And into the river tossed Dick.

Wizard Wozzle

There was once a doleful king whose name was Glum. "Glum by name and glum by nature," his courtiers often said.

At long last, King Glum, fed up with always feeling glum, drew up a royal proclamation: "Half my kingdom to anyone who can make me laugh!"

Now an old out-of-work wizard named Wozzle learned of the king's vow and decided that with the aid of magic he could make the king laugh. He read one book of magic after another until at last on the thirteenth page of the thirteenth volume he read the following:

"Take half a cupful of laughing gas and mix well with a maiden's giggle. Add a table spoonful of a monkey's chuckle and a pickpocket's cunning grin. Serve hot with a nudge in the ribs."

Not such an easy recipe to fulfil even for a wizard like Wozzle. It took him thirteen years to gather together all the ingredients. Then breathlessly he hurried to the palace of King Glum.

"Your Majesty," he gasped, hurrying towards the king, "it's taken me years and years . . ." At that moment he tripped over his beard, bumped into the Lord High Chamberlain, who crashed into the Captain of the Guard, who reeled and cannoned into the Queen, knocking her out of the window into the freezing cold moat. King Glum who didn't like his Queen, laughed for the first time in his life and gave half his kingdom to Wizard Wozzle.

Just ducky

On the opposite page you can read how Farmer Dick tickled his bull with a stick and landed up in the river. Well, as he was clambering out, Dim Dan the pie-shop man who happened to be passing asked him how many ducks he kept on the farm.

Farmer Dick scowled.

"Fancy asking me such a stupid question just now! Can't you see I'm wet through? But, as it happens, this morning as my ducks ran down the path I saw there was a duck in front of two ducks, a duck behind two ducks and a duck between two ducks. So, Dim Dan, how many ducks have I?"

"Just for once I know the answer," cackled Dim Dan. "*Three*! One after the other."

Farmer Dick was cold and wet and angry that Dim Dan knew the right answer, so he kicked Dan into the river too.

Tim the tinker

Tim Tappit was a tinker and made his living repairing old pots and pans. Very proud of his trade he was and known far and wide for all the questions he asked about other people's trades. For instance, what trade has a man whose best works are always trampled on? Why, a shoemaker. Then again, of what trade is a preacher at a wedding? A joiner. And of what trade can it be said that all its members are men of letters? The printing trade. What trade does the Prime Minister follow? Cabinet-maker.

Now one day, Tim Tappit was strolling along the highway when, lying in a ditch at the side of the road, he happened to see an old copper dish.

"H'm," thought he, "that looks a *very* old dish. It might be worth a lot of money."

While cleaning the dish later, he noticed some lettering engraved on its side. "This is the dish in which Oliver Cromwell cooked King Charles's goose," it read.

"Fancy that!" gasped Tim and next day sold the dish for a hundred pounds. Lucky Tim!

The mouse hunt

Paul and Polly and Jane and Robert and Tommy and George and Amanda were seven very nice children, but none of them – not one single one of them had ever seen a mouse!

Just fancy that!

Never seen a mouse!

One day Mrs. Brown, who was the mother of Paul, Polly and Jane, said: "I will take you three and Robert and Tommy and George and Amanda into the country. We will have a picnic and see if we can see any mice."

And that is what they did, and they found this field you can see in the picture.

And while Mrs. Brown had a nice rest on the other side of the big tree, Paul and Polly and Jane and Robert and Tommy and George and Amanda all looked for mice. Robert even had a map, but it wasn't much help.

But in the end, they did find seven mice hidden round the field.

See how many *you* can find.

A little brown mouse

Now here on this page you will all clearly see
An artist has painted a picture of me.
But why do you think that the artist-man
    chose
A little brown mouse and a wayside rose?

He might have chosen a sunset at sea
Or maybe a view with a beautiful tree,
But he got out his paints and I started to pose –
A little brown mouse and a wayside rose.

Perhaps I'll be famous and all will agree
The artist was right in deciding on me.
"How charming!" they'll cry. "Such a cute
    little nose!"
That little brown mouse and a wayside rose!

I was pleased to oblige and I won't charge a fee,
I said the artist could paint me for free,
But why he should ask me I cannot suppose –
A little brown mouse and a wayside rose.

Wilfred's bananas

Wilfred was a little boy who had just reached the age when he was tall enough to put his hands on the tops of high tables and take off everything he could feel. It also meant he could *see* all the things on low tables.

Wilfred thought that being as tall as this was wonderful.

Now that he could reach all the interesting things on table tops, there were so many more things for him to play with!

However, Wilfred's mummy and daddy were not quite so pleased.

They thought it was a nuisance that their young son could reach everything on all the tables.

"Now we have to take everything off the tables and put them on high shelves," they complained.

To little Wilfred it really was a mystery. "I don't see why they have to do that at all," he thought. "All I want to do with those things is chew and lick and bounce them. What's wrong with that?"

One day, Wilfred was going to have bananas for tea, so his mother put them in a bowl and put the bowl on a table. "If Wilfred takes one it won't matter," she said.

Wilfred was thrilled. He reached for the bananas at once. But can you guess what he did? He chewed the bowl and played football with the bananas and then he just couldn't understand why Mummy was so cross and angry with him.

"Grown-ups are *funny*," he mumbled.

21

The jolly robin

One day a robin and a wren perched on a branch above some pretty bluebells.

"Hallo, Jenny," chirped the robin.

The wren frowned.

"My name is Esmeralda," she said haughtily, "so I assume you are not talking to me."

"Oh dear, sorry," chirped the robin in reply, "but I thought all wrens were called Jenny Wren, so naturally, I thought you were called Jenny."

The wren looked back coldly.

"Well, if all wrens were called Jenny, that would be pretty stupid. We should all get into a terrible muddle and no one would ever know which of us was which."

Actually the robin couldn't help thinking that as all wrens *looked* exactly alike, no one could tell which of them was which anyway. But he felt it might not be quite polite to say so.

"Anyway," went on the wren, "if you were speaking to me, what did you want to say?"

"Oh," grinned the robin, who did like a joke, "I was going to ask you if you had heard the story about the peacock."

"No, I haven't" said the wren. "What is it?"

"Well, you should listen to it some time," grinned the robin. "It's a beautiful tale."

He waited in vain for the wren to laugh.

"That's a sort of pun about *story* meaning *tale* and peacocks having beautiful *tails*," he explained.

"Very interesting," smiled the wren. "Tell me, is your name Mr. Redbreast?"

Tom, Tom

Tom, Tom, the piper's son, stole a pig and away did run! Goodness! I always thought that meant that Tom stole the pig and ran away with it in his arms.

But of course!

Looking at this picture it's plain to see that Tom got the *pig* to run away and then *he* rode on *its* back.

How very clever!

But as it turned out, on this day the pig was even cleverer than Tom.

"I think you had better take me home again, Tom," grunted the pig, "or I shall have to arrest you."

Tom laughed. "How can a pig arrest me?" he grinned.

"Oh, that's easy," grunted the pig, "I'm not a pig at all, I'm a police dog in disguise."

And do you know, silly Tom believed him.

Butterflies

Chubby, the lion cub, put his paw into the stream and tried to catch a fish which was dozing in the sun-warmed water.

But the fish wasn't as sleepy as all that, and it quickly squirmed out of reach.

"Perhaps if you asked the fish a riddle it would come closer to listen and then you could catch it," suggested the butterflies, who never could mind their own business.

Chubby peered down into the stream.

"What is everyone doing at the same time?" he called to the fish.

"Growing older," bubbled the fish, without coming one inch nearer to Chubby's paw. "And as I intend to go on growing older, I'm off before you can catch me. Goodbye!"

"Well, your idea wasn't very good," said Chubby to the butterflies.

"Now, don't be cross," replied the butterflies. "After all, we *are* related. Lions are *cats* and we come from *cat*erpillars. Goodbye!"

The lost football

One day Terry Tortoise was walking past a well, when he saw a crow, a pig, a hare and a duck all heaving hard on the well rope.

"That must be a jolly heavy bucket of water you boys are pulling up," he remarked, because all the creatures were puffing and panting mightily.

"Well, it's not so much the water as our friend, Jumbo," panted the crow. "You see, we lost our football down the well and Jumbo leaned over to look for it, and he fell in. So now we are having to pull up the bucket and Jumbo and the football as well, we hope."

Terry Tortoise grinned.

"When Jumbo gets to the top ask him why it is that elephants are always ready to go on long holidays," he said.

"Well, why is it that elephants are always ready to go on long holidays?" asked the pig.

"Because they always have their trunks with them," chuckled Terry Tortoise.

Just then Jumbo and the football and the bucket of water came safely over the side of the well.

The animals who had been pulling on the rope were very hot, so they all had a long drink of the water.

"Here's a riddle for you, Terry," smiled the hare. "Why do we drink water?"

"Because there's no need to chew it," replied Terry. He was a clever fellow.

23

A prince there was

A prince there was who one fine day,
While riding out upon his way,
Espied a maiden, bright and gay,
Her name was Isabella May.

Her clothes were rags, her beauty fair,
And long and golden was her hair.
Then coronets and jewels rare
The prince threw at her feet so bare.

"I'm deep in love with thee," said he.
"Accept these riches now from me!"
The maiden smiled and then said she
"My love I will not sell to thee!"

"But if my love you want to hold,"
The girl went on in tones so bold,
"You see my feet so sore and cold?
"You'll win my heart with *shoes* – not gold!"

The prince did smile! Without delay
He married her that very day.

Sleepy Sammy

"Wakey-wakey, Sammy. When is a boy not a boy?" called out Sammy's mummy.

"When he's a-bed!" replied Sammy sleepily. Sammy had got up once that morning, washed, dressed and had breakfast, but was so sleepy he had crept back to bed again. Do *you* ever do that?

"Come on, Sammy. Stir yourself," smiled his mummy, "and tell me what question can never be answered by 'Yes' "

Sammy grinned. " 'Are you asleep?' of course," he replied. "I say, Mummy, what is it that has four legs and only one foot? Bet you don't know."

"You're right. I don't know," admitted his mummy.

"Why, a bedstead! Caught you that time," laughed cheeky Sammy.

"Yes and I've caught you too," laughed his mummy, taking hold of his collar. "Now come along, sonny-boy. Time for school!"

Fergus the frog

Duke Fergus, the young and handsome ruler of the dukedom of Dillydown was at his wits' end. While seeking to drive an evil magician, Black Guthrun, from his dukedom, he has been taken unawares by the magician who had turned him into a frog!

"And a frog you'll remain until your fingers touch Fairy Gold," he had sneered.

Forlorn and friendless, Fergus hopped along through the dark depths of the Forest of Gloom. Suddenly a faint breeze whispering through the leaves of a rose-bush seemed to sigh: "In the castle of Gertrude the Giantess you will find Fairy Gold."

Scarcely believing his ears, but hoping he had heard aright, Fergus at once made his way to the castle of the mighty giantess Gertrude whom everyone feared.

Now Gertrude had a secret fear. For some strange reason she was afraid of...*frogs*! That was why as soon as she saw Fergus, she fled from her castle. Delightedly, Fergus hopped from room to room until at last he came to a huge treasure chest. Throwing it open, he dipped his "hands" into the fairy Gold. At once he was again the young and handsome Duke Fergus.

Meanwhile Gertrude had met Guthrun, quarrelled with him dreadfully, and furiously chased him from the dukedom.

Flower-potty

Little Freda Fribbles was potty about flowers. All day long she would potter about the garden, planting a flower here, digging up a weed there.

"There's nothing wrong with loving flowers, but I do wish Freda would make friends with other children too," her mummy would say.

Then one day Freda came rushing into the house, her face alight with excitement.

"Mummy! Mummy!" she cried. "Look!" But her mummy waved her aside.

"Don't bother me now, Freda," she said unhappily, and Freda saw that there were tears in her mummy's eyes.

"Oh, Mummy – what's the matter?" gasped Freda. "What's happened?"

"I've lost my wedding ring somewhere," wept her mummy. "Oh dear, I'm so unhappy."

"Cheer up, Mummy. I've just dug up your wedding ring in the garden," cried Freda, producing the missing ring. From then on her mummy was *always* happy to see Freda pottering in the garden.

The greedy Emperor

Once upon a time, long ago and far away in the land of burning desert sands and tall rocky windswept mountains, there lived a very greedy emperor. He loved dressing in fine clothes and wearing beautiful jewels, but he didn't want anyone else to do so.

He took so much money in taxes from his subjects that even his palace officials dressed in rags and had no fine jewellery.

One day his chief adviser came and asked for permission to wear a fine jewel at his daughter's wedding.

The emperor was amazed to learn that the adviser had a jewel left. "My tax collectors must be getting lazy," he thought. "Where did you get the jewel?" he asked.

"Oh," said the adviser, "don't be angry. I have no money left, but in my family we know of a deep dark cave. If a man ventures there alone at midnight and says: 'Cave, cave, so dark and deep, give to me a jewel to keep,' and leaves a gift of oatcakes, a jewel will be put in his hand. That is how I came by this jewel."

There wasn't a word of truth in the story, but the greedy emperor so loved jewels, he couldn't resist the idea of getting a jewel in return for oatcakes. He made his adviser show him the cave and at midnight he went in there carrying his oatcakes. At once the adviser and his friends blocked the entrance to the cave. The emperor was trapped and try as he may, he could not get out.

Then they went to the palace and taking back all their own money and a little bit extra they fled to a distant country where the emperor wasn't so greedy. When their emperor had at last dug his way out of the cave, he was a poorer but much wiser man.

Timothy at the seaside

One year, when Timothy Timpletumkins was very young, he went to the seaside for the first time.

He couldn't believe his eyes when he saw the sea.

"What a lot of water!" he gasped.

He couldn't think where it had all come from or why it was never still.

Timothy was taken down to the beach and dressed in a swimming costume and told he could play on the sand.

"But you mustn't go into the sea until Daddy has changed into a swimsuit and can go in with you," he was told.

Timothy looked at the restless sea slapping and swirling about on the sand. He just touched it with one toe and found that it was *freezing*. "Don't worry," he thought "I shan't be going into *that*."

And Timothy had a lovely time playing on the warm sand and making sandpies. "I'll leave the sea to the grown-ups," he smiled.

Mary's lamb

Mary had a little lamb,
Its fleece was white as snow,
And everywhere that Mary went,
The lamb was sure to go.

Mary had a little doll,
Which could both smile and talk.
She liked to brush its yellow hair,
And take it for a walk.

Everywhere that Mary went
She never walked alone.
She took her lamb and doll along,
And then they all went home.

The archer

Once upon a time there was a boy called Robin who had read all the stories about brave Robin Hood.

"How thrilling it would be to live in the greenwood like Robin Hood", he said to himself one day.

Then he thought again: "Well, why shouldn't *I*? Mummy could make me a splendid Robin Hood outfit, and I needn't actually *live* in the greenwood. I could just go to the wood at the end of the lane on Saturdays and holidays and then go home for supper. Of course, I wouldn't use sharp arrows in case I hurt something – I would use safe arrows with suction caps stuck on the end."

So, every Saturday and every holiday, that is what young Robin did.

He had great fun in the greenwood at the end of the lane, and soon everyone in the neighbourhood called him "The Archer".

One day Robin decided he would try to do something really difficult. With one of his "safe" arrows he would try to hit a frog in mid-leap.

Robin went to the pond at the end of the greenwood. A frog was about to leap from a water-lily pad. Robin took aim.

"What are you doing?" croaked the startled frog?

"I'm Robin Hood and I'm trying to hit you with an arrow," said Robin.

"Well," said the clever, quick-witted frog, "I'm your king, Richard Lionheart, returning from the crusades in disguise. You cannot shoot *me*."

And Robin didn't.

28

The two bears

Barney Bear and Woodstock Bear lived in different parts of the same forest. One day they met. "Good morning, my name is Barney," smiled Barney Bear.

"*Barmy* Bear," grinned Woodstock. "Well, I must say you are well named. You look quite barmy to me with only one strap to your trousers, silly hat and that funny looking rope with two knots in it."

"I said Bar*ney* not Bar*my*," growled Barney, realising it wasn't a morning for being polite. "You don't have to tell me *your* name. I only have to see that piece of wood in your hand to know that you are the crazy bear they call Woodstock – the very silly bear that stocks up wood outside his cave."

"Collecting wood isn't so silly," Woodstock replied. "One day wood might become scarce. Then I shall be glad of it to make fires to keep me warm in cold weather."

"Run short of wood? In a forest of ten thousand square miles?" laughed Barney. "Not very likely, is it?"

"All right then," said Woodstock. "Why are you carrying that knotted rope then?"

"The knots are to remind me of things. But I can't remember what things," said Barney.

"I was right about your name the first time," said Woodstock.

Mr. Mouse's riddles

Mr. Mouse and Mrs. Mouse and their three little mouselets lived in a hay house in the corner of an old barn.

Now Mr. Mouse was very fond of asking riddles. He would ask: "What makes more noise than a trombone?"

The answer was – two trombones?

Then Mr. Mouse would ask: "Why is a pack of cards like a garden shed?"

The answer was: "Because there are spades in it. Isn't that good?"

To tell the truth, *Mrs*. Mouse did not care much for riddles. She thought they were silly and that Mr. Mouse would be better employed searching around for food or keeping an eye on the farm cat.

However, Mrs. Mouse didn't complain – until they had three baby mice.

"Now, Daddy Mouse," said Mrs. Mouse, "I want you to stop asking all those riddles. I don't want the children to grow up asking riddles like their father. It will annoy their teachers when they go to school and we don't want that to happen, do we?"

"You mean I must stop asking: 'What is the worst weather for rats and mice?' – 'When it is raining cats and dogs?' and 'What never uses its teeth to eat?' – 'A comb!' " groaned Mr. Mouse.

"That's exactly what I mean", replied Mrs. Mouse.

So for the sake of the children, Mr. Mouse stopped asking riddles and life became very dull.

But the day came when the mouselets started speaking in whole sentences. One day one mouselet looked at the railway track which ran near the barn.

"What is a twack?" he asked.

Mrs. Mouse looked surprised. "Twack? Twack? I don't know what a twack is."

But another mouselet said: "A twack is what a twain wuns on."

Of course, they were talking baby talk but Mr. Mouse thought they were making an attempt at asking riddles. He was pleased.

"If the mouselets ask riddles without being taught, it must be right for them," he said and started telling riddles again.

Mrs. Mouse was furious – the mouselets were delighted!

Squirrel gifts

Once upon a time there were two naughty little squirrels.

There were far, far naughtier than any little girl or boy would dream of being.

Tinker and Scamp their friends called them, because they were always such little tinkers and such little scamps.

One of the things Tinker and Scamp liked doing best was eating their favourite nuts and then throwing the shells at anyone unlucky enough to be passing by.

Then one day a very nice little girl called Sarah came walking in the woodland where Tinker and Scamp lived.

Now, Sarah was the kindest little girl you can imagine and she always thought the best of everyone.

So when naughty Tinker and Scamp threw the shells of their nuts at her, which of course they did, Sarah said: "What dear squirrels you are. Thank you for giving me such nice gifts. I will paint these shells and make a necklace."

"Goodness!" gasped Tinker and Scamp. "We've been good without meaning to be. It feels quite nice! We must be good more often."

The horn of Gareth

Long ago in olden days, there were no telephones, no radios, no postmen.

If someone wanted to call people together, a messenger had to go round telling them when they were to meet.

It took a long time and was often very inconvenient, as well as dangerous, because in those days, there were no policemen either, and thieves and robbers roamed the land.

But then a young man named Gareth, who was fond of music, made a magnificent horn. It was so loud and clear that a blast on it would carry far across his valley.

And Gareth said that whenever good men and true had to gather together to right a wrong, he would blow on his horn. And all honest men would answer Gareth's call and their valley became a fine place to live.

31

Rosebud cheeks

One birthday, a little girl called Molly was given a doll with rosy cheeks.

"What are you going to call her?" her mummy asked before Molly had even had time to get to know the doll at all.

"Rosy Cheeks," whispered Molly, because she couldn't think of anything else.

But when she undressed her dolly she found the name 'Rosebud' written on her vest.

"Hello, Rosebud Cheeks!" said Molly.

The cornfield

When you are out in the country and you pass a field of growing corn, you probably won't notice any living creatures at all.

You will just see the beautiful corn rippling in the wind.

But among the corn there are *hundreds* of living creatures.

There are rabbits and mice and spiders and beetles, not to mention worms and birds.

Here is a picture of a little fieldmouse whose home is in the cornfield.

"Which is the furriest side of a mouse?" he is asking.

"The *out*side, of course!"

The treasure

On Friday evening David watched a really *exciting* film on television.

It was about wicked pirates who robbed ships of gold and jewels and buried all their stolen treasure on a far island in the south seas.

Years later, when only two of the pirates were left alive, they went back and dug up their treasure and took it back to England. They were rich, but unhappy, men for the rest of their lives, for every night they had nightmares about all the people they had robbed.

"Those were exciting days!" murmured David. "Still the evenings must have been pretty boring without television."

The glove

Long ago, manners and customs were very different.

No well dressed lady, for example, would dream of going out without wearing gloves.

Even in summer ladies and gentlemen always wore gloves.

They even wore gloves when they went to parties and dances. It was thought the proper thing to do.

So you can imagine how dreadful a young lady felt one day. She left home in a hurry, snatching up her gloves as she went only to find that she had picked up a single glove. She had left the other lying on the hall table.

There was no time to go back to fetch the glove. But she couldn't possibly meet her friends, wearing only *one glove*. They would be most disapproving.

But luckily for the young lady, her little sister came running after her with the glove. She had found it on the table and had guessed what had happened.

So the young lady was able to continue happily on her way, and have a lovely time with her friends. She was so grateful to her kind little sister that she brought her home a basket of strawberries as a thank you present.

Bath time

One day Humpty Dumpty was on his way to sit on a wall, when an old woman who lived in a coal scuttle stopped him.

"I want to bath my dog and my cat today," she said. "But I can't manage on my own. Will you help me?"

Now Humpty Dumpty certainly didn't want to help with a messy job like that, so he said – "I will help if you can answer this riddle. What gets wetter, the more it dries?"

"A *towel* of course," replied the old woman. So Humpty Dumpty had to help her – and it did save him from falling off the wall that day.

Drummer boy

Nobody in all the land was prouder than Jimmy Jingle the day he became a regimental drummer boy. Now a drummer's life is a busy one and the only time that Jimmy had to practise was early in the morning.

So early every morning, Jimmy strapped on his drum and drummed and drummed. *DRRRRum! DRRRRum! Drum! Drum!*

Several days went by. Then the General sent for Jimmy.

"Jingle!" he roared. "You wake me up every morning with your drumming. Enough is too much! Your drumming must cease! So stop it – at once! Immediately! Understand?"

Jimmy understood.

"Oh dear!" he sighed, as he left the General's headquarters. "If I'm not allowed to practise and practise, I'll never be chosen to play my drum on the Queen's birthday."

He needn't have worried. Three days later the General sent for him again.

"Jingle!" he roared. "Without your early drumming, I'm over-sleeping. I've been late for parade these last three mornings. I order you to drum outside my bedroom window every morning." Jimmy did – *and* he played his drum on the Queen's birthday.

Who's for tea?

A fox there lurks behind a tree,
Waiting very patiently.
He listens for a quack or cluck
For that will mean a hen or duck!

That fox that stands so silently
Is waiting for his tea you see.
Some thoughtless bird may come – and then
It's duck for tea – or maybe hen!

On whom, we ask, will fall good luck?
On hungry fox – or hen – or duck?

Which bee?

"Hurrah! Here we go again!" whooped Binky Bear as he spotted a bees' nest high up in a tree. "That honey's for me!"

In two shakes of a bear's tail, young Binky was up that tree and reaching out a paw to scoop out some honey. As he did so, an angry bee stung him.

"YOW!" yelled Binky, and scrambling down the tree ran back to his mother.

"Hey, Mum! One of those nasty bees stung me just as I was helping myself to some of their honey," he wailed.

"How many times have I told you to stay away from bees' nests?" demanded his mother. But there was twinkle in her eye. "Now, Binky, if you'll just point out to me which bee stung you, I'll give it a good scolding."

But that was more than Binky could do!

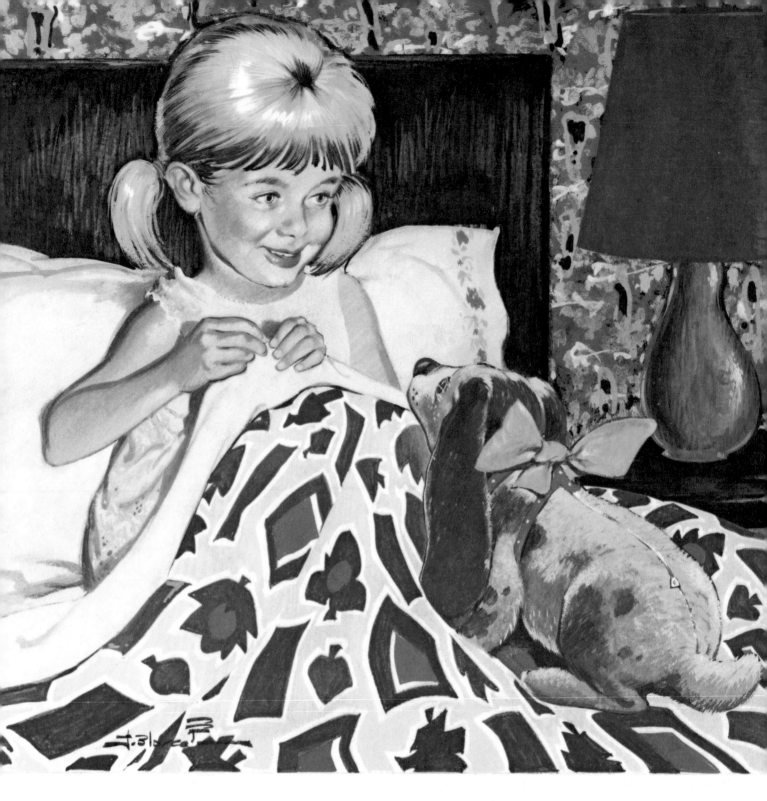

The lonely toy dog

Katy was the youngest in her family.

She had a brother and a sister, but they were much older than she was.

Her sister was married and her brother was away at school.

Now Katy's brother, Bobby, had been given a toy dog when he was little.

It was a cuddly little thing and sat on Bobby's bed with Bobby's pyjamas zipped up inside it.

But, of course, when Bobby went away to school, Spotty, the toy dog, sat all alone on Bobby's bed.

Spotty looked lonely on the empty bed with no one to talk to him and no one to snuggle up to at night.

Katy felt very sorry for Spotty, and one day she said to her mother: "Don't you think it would be nice, while Bobby is away at school, if Spotty came into *my* room and lived on *my* bed?"

And Mummy said that was quite a good idea, so long as Spotty went back into Bobby's room when he came home.

But when Bobby came home, he said: "Thank you, for being kind to Spotty. He is yours now."

Mummy's card

It was Mummy's birthday and little Tim had already been out with Grandma to buy her a present. But Tim wanted to give Mummy something else, something that he had made himself with no grown-up help at all.

So little Tim decided to paint Mummy a birthday card.

He took his paints and went into the garden and painted a picture of the big, leafy chestnut tree.

Tim thought his picture was pretty good – a little smudgy perhaps, but then nothing is perfect, as Tim was always hearing Mummy say when her cooking went a little wrong and Daddy remarked on it.

Then little Tim remembered that cards are supposed to have writing on them. But of course he couldn't write yet, so he decided to ask his mother a riddle instead.

He gave Mummy the card and said: "Do you know what can jump higher than a tree?"

"Oh, nothing can jump higher than a tree," laughed Mummy.

Tim grinned. "*I* can," he cried, "because a tree can't jump."

How Mummy did laugh and when Daddy came home she told him Tim's joke.

Greedy Billy

There was once a family of nine baby bluetits. They were born in the nesting-box in Timothy's garden. They were a very noisy family, and especially when the parents brought food home.

Now, apart from being noisy, eight of the babies were very well behaved. But Billy was very naughty indeed and he was also *greedy!* It was because of Billy that his parents were pleased when the time came for the babies to leave the nest and begin to fend for themselves.

Billy was pleased too. Now he could do and eat, exactly what he liked. He began by eating some juicy blackberries. Bluetits do not usually eat blackberries because they not agree with them, but Billy thought they were delicious! First he ate the ripe black ones – then he ate the red *unripe* ones – then he began to feel ill.

When it was time for his evening flying lesson, Billy's family came to look for him but didn't feel like flying.

"Now perhaps that will teach you not to be so greedy!" his mother scolded. And do you know, Billy wasn't greedy again – not even when his tummy-ache had disappeared.

Ellie Elephant

Ellie the elephant loved to invite her friends round for a chat and a joke.

One day she invited Michael Mouse, Mary Mole, Peregrine Pelican, who wasn't often invited out, because so few people could say his name properly, Boris Bear, who wasn't often invited either, because he would keep telling the same story over and over again, and Tommy Toucan.

Ellie made them all a lovely tea of pineapples, cherries, apples, oranges and other beautiful fruit.

Ellie started off by asking a riddle. "What animal is most like an elephant?" she asked.

"Another elephant," grinned Boris Bear. "My turn now! Have you heard the story about the broken pencil?"

"Don't bother to tell it," grinned Peregrine Pelican. "There's no point."

Mike Mouse was dancing round the room with Mandy Mole. "Do you know what you call a mouse after it's a year old?" he asked her.

"No. I don't know," replied Mandy.

"Two years old," squeaked Mike.

Then it was time for Tommy Toucan to join in. He had a bird riddle. "Why do little birds in the nest agree?" he asked.

"Because they are afraid of falling out," replied Peregrine Pelican, who of course, knew all about birds.

Then all the friends sat down to eat the lovely fruit Ellie had bought for them. "Which is the best side of a pineapple?" asked Ellie.

"The inside," giggled Mandy Mole.

Prince Jester

There was once a shy Prince who fell in love with a beautiful Princess. He was so sure she wouldn't notice him among all the other princes that, when he heard a jester was wanted at the Palace to dance, sing and make everyone happy, he dressed himself up and went along for the job. He was a great success at making everyone happy and was so kind that soon everyone loved him, *including* the Princess. "If only you were a prince I could marry you!" she sighed. "But I am," he said forgetting to be shy. Soon after they were happily married.

Jokey Bird

Being a wild animal isn't always fun. Wild animals can't call a doctor if they don't feel very well, or buy ointment from the chemist if they have a sore back.

Now it is a fact that rhinoceros have little insects living on their backs, which irritate them greatly. As they can't go to a doctor or the chemist, they have to rely on birds which come and perch on their backs and peck off the insects one by one.

This works very well, because the birds get a meal and the rhinos get rid of the insects as well as getting their backs scratched.

But there was one bird who wasn't content with eating insects, he would tell jokes as well — the same jokes over and over and over again.

He nearly drove the rhinos mad, but they had to put up with him because he was such a good insect eater.

So that's why being a wild animal isn't always fun. They never hear any new jokes!

Happy rabbit

Happy little bunny rabbit,
Had a very lucky habit.
Every day he would awake,
Long before the dawn did break.
Out into the fields he'd go,
While his brothers snored below.
So the best of food he'd eat,
Which he thought was pretty neat.

Skippy Jane

Skippy Jane Whiskers who loves skipping was laughing and skipping at the same time one day. Mrs. Tabby Tibbles wondered why. "That naughty kitcat Timmy Paddypaws came home with his new suit covered in mud," said Jane. "And how did that happen?" asked Mrs. Tibbles. "Do you see that muddy ditch over there?" grinned Jane. "Yes," replied Mrs. Tibbles. "Well, Timmy didn't," laughed Jane.

Breakfast with Bertie

Breakfast with Bertie Biggles is always good fun. For instance, the other morning his Daddy asked him. "What did you learn at school yesterday, Bertie?" And Bertie said. "I learned what kind of shoes are made from banana skins. SLIPPERS! He! He! He! Teacher also told me why King John never drew a straight line. It was because he was a bad ruler. Tell me, Daddy, what animal has spots and lives at the South Pole?"

"Could it be a leopard that has lost its way?" Bertie's Daddy asked. "Talking about the South Pole, what is the difference between the North Pole and the South Pole?"

"All the difference in the world," said Bertie.

"Which reminds me. Why can't you travel to the four corners of the world?" Mummy and Daddy shook their heads. "Because the world is round," Bertie told them.

"Clever boy," smiled Daddy. "Now, Bertie, why were you late for school the other day?"

"Well," replied Bertie, "as I was on my way I saw a notice which read 'School ahead. Go slow.' So I went slow! When I arrived Lizbeth Little was lisping lengthy lessons. How many times can you say 'Lizbeth Little lisps lengthy lessons' without making a mistake, Mummy?" Bertie's mummy tried and tried and Bertie and his daddy laughed and laughed. And then Daddy tried, and Mummy laughed, too.

Gipsy Bunny

Not a care in the world has Gipsy Bunny as he rattles along the road in his gaily painted caravan, drawn by his faithful horse Dobbin. "Hey there, Dobbin," calls out Gipsy Bunny. "How can it be proved that you have six legs? Why, because you have forelegs in front and two legs behind. And why are you the most unusual feeder of all animals? You don't know the answer to that either, do you? It's because you eat best when there isn't a bit in your mouth. Did you hear about the horse that ate an electric wire instead of hay? No? Well, it went haywire? Do you know why that pony we saw this morning couldn't talk? Because it's a little horse. *Hoarse*, see? And why is an ice-cream like a horse? The more you lick it, the faster it goes!"

Sweet Sue

An Indian girl called Sweet Sue
One day made her way to the zoo.
And while she was there,
She saw a wee bear
Who said "I like you – I do!"

"Is that so?" then giggled Sweet Sue.
"Well, Bruin, here's what I will do.
"I'll buy you for me
"And then home to tea
"Will go me and lovable you!"

"How much for young Bruin?" asked Sue
"Five beads," smiled the keeper, "to you!"
Her necklace she swopped
And the bear did adopt,
And carried him home from the zoo.

Mittens, Moppett and Muffin

Princess Patience was beautiful. Her parents the King and Queen had long hoped that their beautiful daughter would meet, fall in love with and marry a handsome prince who was also good and kind. But alas, Princess Patience seemed to have no time for princes good, kind or otherwise. All she had time for were her three pet kittens, Mittens, Moppett and Muffin, whom she loved dearly.

"But Patience *must* marry some day," the King would often say to the Queen, "for she is our only child and there is no male heir to the throne."

But Patience did not heed her parents' pleas—until one morning when Mittens, Moppett and Muffin went missing! Servants and noblemen searched everywhere for the lost kittens, but Mittens, Moppet and Muffin remained lost: no one could find them.

"Whoever finds my kittens and brings them to me safe and sound, I'll . . . I'll *marry*," vowed the Princess at last.

Now, what Princess Patience did not know was that the kittens' mother belonged to Gawain, a handsome young man who worked in the kitchen. The kittens had grown tired of being the playthings of a selfish princess and had gone home to their mother. When Gawain heard of the Princess's vow, he took the kittens back to her at once.

How delighted she was to see her kittens again, but how furious that she would have to marry a common servant! She had to keep her promise of course. But although Gawain was not a prince, he was good and kind and made the Princess happy to the end of her days.

Griselda Giraffe

Griselda and Gerald were two little giraffes who lived with their parents in the heart of the jungle.

Gerald was a happy-go-lucky young fellow, always ready for fun and games. Griselda, on the other hand, was a very proud young creature – so proud in fact that even the thought of lowering her head was too much for her. When she was thirsty she refused to put her head down alongside Gerald's. Instead, she drank water from the pool through a hollow cane, just as humans drink lemonade through a straw.

Then one day, Griselda decided that she was far too proud to play with Gerald any longer. Poor Gerald! Griselda was his only friend.

"You should remember that pride goes before a *fall*," he said, as Griselda stalked away.

"Nonsense!" Griselda replied, tossing her head. But Griselda was not looking where she was going. Suddenly she found herself falling headlong into a deep pit. She tried and tried to scramble out. But the pit was too deep. Pride *had* indeed gone before a fall.

At last, as night began to fall, Griselda began to cry for help, for she was afraid of the dark.

It was Gerald who came to her rescue. In his mouth, he carried Griselda's drinking cane. He lowered it into the pit. "Grip it in your teeth and I'll pull you out," said he. A grateful Griselda was never proud again.

Sandy's day

Sandy was a little puppy who led a very busy life.

He would wake up in the morning and peer out from under the warm blanket in his cosy basket.

Then he would trot across to his mistress and beg for his breakfast.

Sandy had soon learnt that if he begged nicely he could get almost anything he wanted.

After breakfast, Sandy would spend a pleasant hour or so patrolling round the garden and chasing next door's cat.

After that it was time for a nap on the best cushion – when no one was looking of course!

Then after another meal, Sandy would find time to bury a slipper. The family did have *such* fun looking for it. Or so Sandy thought.

Then it was time to take little master for a walk. The exercise did him so much good.

Later on, it was time for yawning and snuggling down again in that nice comfy basket.

What a busy day!

Growing up

Lisa was a very pretty little girl with long golden hair. Lisa loved pretty clothes and she had one summer dress which was her particular favourite.

The dress was white with a blue collar and had little bluebells printed all over it.

Lisa wore the dress whenever she could. She only did not wear it when her mother said it must be washed.

But of course, winter came, as it always does and the weather was too cold for summer dresses. Lisa had to wear warm jumpers and skirts.

All through the winter Lisa never forgot her pretty bluebell dress and when the first hot summer day came, she asked her mother: "Please Mummy, may I wear my pretty bluebell dress?"

Mummy took the summer dress from the high shelf where it had been all winter and gave it to Lisa to put on.

Oh *DEAR*!

The dress was far too *small*!

Lisa had grown so much she could hardly get into the dress. The buttons would not fasten and she looked quite *ridiculous*.

"Ah well," sighed Mummy. "You *are* growing up, aren't you!"

Lisa was sad about her dress, but pleased to think she was *growing up*. Then Mummy made the dress into a blouse and all that summer a happy Lisa wore her pretty bluebell blouse.

The new house

Bang! Bang! Bang!

Mr. Carpenter was helping to build a new house.

"What doesn't mind being hit on the head?" he called to his little son, who was watching him.

"A nail, of course," grinned the boy.

"And what knows everything these planks of wood did yesterday?" went on the carpenter.

"Your saw," grinned the boy, "because it saw-ed them."

"Why do you know the answers to all my riddles?" asked the carpenter.

"Because you have asked them all before," grinned the little boy, "but I still like hearing them."

45

The Yule log

In case you have never seen one before, the big log in this picture is called a Yule log.

In olden days before central heating or electric fires, people used to go out before Christmas and fetch in from the woodlands the biggest log they could find.

And with it they would make an enormous fire to last all through the Christmas holiday.

When the Yule log burned there was a big fire to gather round and to cook on, and it didn't matter if the snow fell and lay thick on the ground outside.

As well as the big log, these little rabbits have collected wood to start the fire and holly and mistletoe for decorations.

Happy Christmas to them all!

Martin's game

When Martin was a little boy, he made a great discovery.

He discovered that if he pressed the little button on the back door a bell rang inside the house – and even better than that, Mummy came dashing to the back door and opened it.

Martin *was* pleased with himself.

Whenever Martin was playing in the garden and he wanted to speak to Mummy, he just pressed the little button.

In fact sometimes when Martin was playing indoors, he would slip outside just to press the button.

It was such fun to hear the ringing noise and then to see Mummy come running to the door.

Martin couldn't understand why Mummy wasn't so pleased.

"You see, when I hear the doorbell, I think it is the milkman or the electric meter man calling," explained Mummy. "And I come hurrying down – all for nothing."

"All for *nothing*!" gasped Martin indignantly, "It isn't all for nothing at all. *I'm* here."

"Well, what I meant," Mummy went on, "was that *you* could come and find *me* when you want to say something, instead of making me go to the trouble of running all the way from the other end of the house."

"Grown-ups are no fun," thought Martin.

The forgetful pussy

Paula Pussycat had a very bad memory.

"Gosh!", she thought, when she got out of bed one morning. "Now, which goes on first, socks or shoes?"

Luckily she decided to put her socks on first.

Then she sat on the side of the bed thinking: "Am I getting up or am I going to bed?" But as she was feeling hungry, she guessed it must be breakfast time.

So she got up and fried bacon and eggs and made a pot of tea.

"Now, do I put the bacon and eggs on the plate or in the cup?" she wondered. "Or do I put the *tea* on the plate or in the cup?"

This time she was unlucky, for she tried to pour the tea out onto the plate – and that made a fine mess.

By the time Paula had mopped up and finished breakfast, it was quite late.

As well as having a very bad memory, Paula was always late for everything – because she could never remember what she was supposed to be doing.

"I should be called Forgetful Pussycat, instead of Paula Pussycat," she sighed.

But she was such a nice, friendly Pussycat, everyone was very forgiving about her forgetting, even when she was late for a meeting, her friends forgave her.

Emma Mouse

Once upon a time there was a mouse who could talk.

She lived in the house of Mario the ice cream seller and Mario soon became quite accustomed to talking to Emma, the mouse.

But although Emma could talk, she was not very interesting.

Every morning just as Mario was going out, Emma would run up to him and say:

"Don't forget to buy some cheese today."

Emma was rather a greedy mouse.

After a while Mario said: "If you can't think of anything else to say except 'Don't forget to buy some cheese today', you needn't bother to say anything – and what's more I won't buy any cheese either."

So Emma really thought hard and the next morning she asked Mario: "How do you get down off an elephant?"

"I don't know. You slide down, I suppose," replied Mario.

"No," grinned Emma, "you don't get down off an elephant. You get *down* off a *duck*."

And Mario enjoyed Emma's riddle, so much that he went straight to the cheese shop and bought some extra nice cream cheese for supper.

After that Emma asked Mario a riddle every morning and they were both happier.

The kitten

Paul lived in a nice house with a big garden and he had a puppy.

One day when the puppy was indoors, a kitten wandered into the garden.

Paul who was playing in the garden spoke to the kitten: "You had better go, because if my puppy sees you, he will chase you."

But the kitten took no notice of Paul, and went on exploring the garden.

Just at that moment, the puppy ran into the garden *barking*.

In a flash, the kitten vanished.

"Kittens certainly understand puppy talk better than human talk," thought Paul and went inside to tell Mummy.

Old Blossom

Farmer Giles had bought a fine new tractor to help him plough his land.

But also on the farm, he kept Old Blossom, the horse who had pulled the plough in Farmer Giles' father's day.

Then one morning, the tractor broke down and the mechanic said it could not be repaired for a month.

Farmer Giles was in despair because he had to do his ploughing while the weather was right.

So he harnessed Old Blossom to the plough and she ploughed the fields for him. "What would I have done without you, old friend?" smiled Farmer Giles.

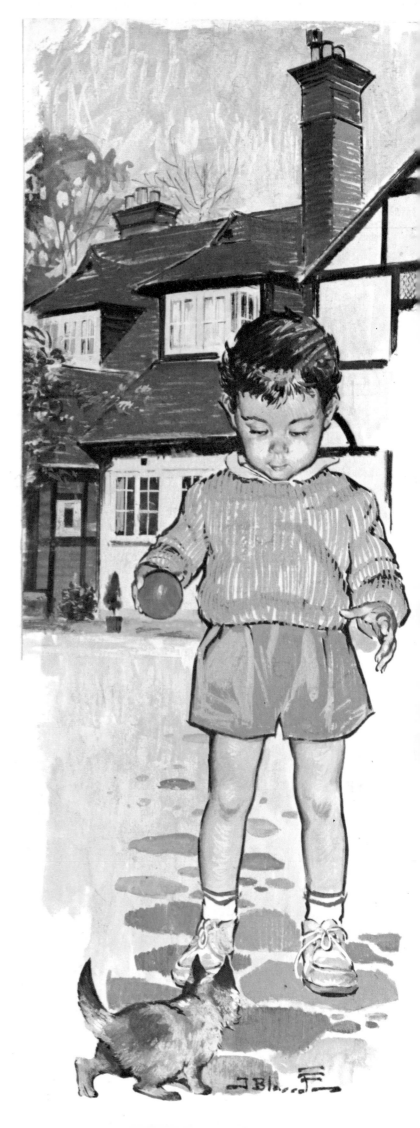

Zebbie Zebra's best time

What time of day do you like best? When you first get up in the morning? No? Eating breakfast, then? Ah, that's better. Going out to play with your best friend? Better still. Going to bed early? *NO!*

The time of day that Zebbie Zebra likes best is when he sits down to read his favourite newspaper. And the best page of his favourite newspaper is the Jokes page.

Here are two of Zebbie's best jokes.

One day a boy answered the front door bell and when he came back, he said to his daddy: "There is a man at the front door with a bald head."

His daddy replied: "Well, send him away – I've already got one."

One silly fellow said to another: "Don't come down the ladder, Jack – I've taken it away." And his chum replied. "Well, put it back quickly – I'm already half-way down!"

The kind sailor

When Jim the sailor came home from the sea, he would bring exciting presents for everybody in his family. One day he didn't notice he had dropped one of his presents. But a poor little boy picked it up, and being very honest, ran after Jim. Jim walked so fast that he had already reached home before the little boy caught up with him.

When the door opened, the boy could see the excited faces of Jim's family and the table spread with food. Jim was so pleased to have the present back he invited the boy in.

"There is plenty here for everyone," he said, "so you must stay."

And the little boy, who did not have a home to go to, stayed with Jim's family that day, and every other day, until he grew up. Then he became a sailor, too.

The young foal

The little foal was born one fine spring day. At first, while she got used to her long legs, she didn't take much notice of anything around her. Then, on the third day, her mother said:

"Off you go for a trot by yourself round the field."

The little foal frisked her tail in the air and scampered off.

First she saw a rabbit. "Hallo, foal," said the rabbit. "Welcome to our beautiful field!"

Then the foal saw a squirrel. "Hallo, foal," said the squirrel. "Welcome to our lovely field!"

Then the foal saw a blackbird who said: "Wel-come to our wonderful field!"

Then the foal saw the bluebells and the new leaves on the trees outside the field. And she thought what a very pretty place she had been born into.

Then the rain started to fall.

"Oh, I don't like this!" she shivered, and sped back to her mother.

The foal snuggled up to her mother. "Look up!" she said. "Even the rain is pretty some-times."

There in the sky was a rainbow. "What a lovely world this is!" said the foal sleepily.

Patrick's new garage

Patrick was given a splendid new car for his birthday. What fun he had racing round the garden. Sometimes he pretended he was a racing driver on a race track. "BRRRRM! BURRRMMMM!" he would shout, as he sped up and down the garden path. But there was one thing that rather spoilt things. His lovely car was too big to be kept indoors, and the garage where his daddy kept *his* car was so full of spades and deck chairs and pots of paint that there was scarcely any room for *his* car and none at all for Patrick's.

So Patrick's car had to be left outside. Then one day, Uncle Tom came to tea. He had no sooner sat down at the tea table than he said: "Oh dear, I forgot to turn off the water-sprinkler in my garden. When I get home the whole garden will be flooded."

Without saying a word, Patrick jumped into his car, raced round to Uncle Tom's house and turned off the sprinkler. Uncle Tom was so pleased that the next day he made a special little garage for Patrick's car. Patrick was so pleased with it.

"One good turn deserves another," he smiled, and winked at his nephew.

The bad hens

Mrs. Mills, the farmer's wife had just collected all the eggs her hens had laid. She was about to shut the hen house door, when she heard her neighbour, Mrs. Green, call to her. Mrs. Green wanted to tell Mrs. Mills about the cakes she had baked that day for her little girl's birthday party. She had left them on the kitchen table to cool.

What neither of them knew was that the hens were now *out* of the hen house and *inside* Mrs. Green's house! The hens had fluttered up onto the kitchen table and were greedily pecking away at all the new cakes.

Mrs. Green *was* cross. But Mrs. Mills gave her all the eggs she had collected to bake more cakes.

"Those naughty hens will have to lay twice as many eggs tomorrow," said she. And believe it or not – they did.

Monty Monkey

Monty Monkey's daddy was a clown in the circus. Monty did not want to be a clown when *he* grew up. He wanted to swing on the flying trapeze. After all, every monkey *loves* to swing from one tree-branch to another.

So Monty made a long rope of leaves and stems and practised very hard every day, flying through the air and landing BUMP! He even wore his trousers out. Can you see the yellow patch his mummy had to sew on?

One day Monty was practising while the circus was going on in the Big Top. Suddenly his rope broke. Instead of going BUMP on the ground, Monty flew up in the air, through the wide open door of the Big Top and plopped into a bucket of whitewash his daddy and the other clowns were using in their clowns' act. How the monkeys laughed to see the baby monkey covered from head to foot in the messy, squelchy whitewash!

When Monty recovered from his surprise, he laughed too! He thought it was very funny and he liked making everyone laugh so much. So he asked his daddy if he could join the other clowns in their act. Of course, Monty's daddy agreed and Monty became a clown after all and was a great favourite with the audience.

Dancing Harriet

Harriet Hippo wanted to be a ballet dancer. She was quite sure she could be a very good ballet dancer, especially if she danced on her toes. Most of Harriet's friends were not as sure as Harriet and they laughed at her behind her back. But Harriet practised and practised her dancing night and day, and night and day the whole jungle shook.

One day news reached the jungle that Lady Gazelle was coming to judge a dancing competition. The first prize was to be a gold cup! All Harriet's friends decided to enter and, of course, so did Harriet. How her friends giggled and laughed to each other. To think that huge Harriet could *possibly* win! "Why," sneered Georgina Giraffe, "she can't even dance on her toes!" Which was true, and that was worrying Harriet.

On the day of the competition, Harriet lined up with all her giggling friends. When her turn came to dance, she was so excited she started to hiccough! And every time she gasped "Hic!" she stood on her toes. Suddenly she gave an extra loud "HIC!" and she was on her toes till the end of her dance. She won the Competition. "Hooray!" she laughed. "A HIC-cup won me a GOLD cup!" Her friends did not laugh.

The hard hat

One day when Professor Poddlepot went home to his house in Africa, the front door was open and tea was laid on the table. "Strange!" he thought. Then he jumped as he saw a large snake on his chair. Quickly he whipped off his hard African hat, clapped it over the snake and sat on it.

Later his little daughter came in and asked: "Why are you sitting on your hat, Daddy?" When the professor told her, she said: "That snake is my skipping rope. I came in a few minutes ago, and as you were not in, I put my skipping rope on the chair and laid tea for you." Professor Poddlepot did laugh.

Peter and the bee

One day Peter Puppy saw a bee for the first time. He gave it a playful pat with his paw.

"Don't *do* that," said the bee crossly. "I'm too busy to play, and if you make me angry I shall have to sting you. That is what bees do when they are annoyed, and I don't want to sting you because I can see you are just a little puppy."

"What is 'sting'?" asked Peter.

"It is something painful," said the bee. "But I'm busy, so don't annoy me."

"Why are you busy?" asked Peter.

"I'm collecting pollen from the flowers to make honey," said the bee, as it darted in and out of the flowers.

"Would *I* like honey?" asked Peter.

"I don't think so," said the bee. "Puppies like to eat biscuits and meat and slippers."

That reminded Peter how hungry he was.

"Goodbye, Bee," he said. "Next time we meet I won't bother you. But one day I would like to taste your honey."

Easter chicks

Auntie May had called at the Twins' house to ask them to stay with her at Easter. She had a farm and the children loved staying with her. Mummy was pleased for the Twins to go, so it was arranged that they would arrive when Easter-time came.

"I mustn't forget these eggs," said Auntie May to Mummy when she thought the Twins were not listening. "They are the children's Easter present." Well, the children *were* disappointed because they knew that the two eggs in the basket were real ones – and not exciting chocolate Easter eggs at all! Also, Easter was weeks away. Surely the eggs would be bad by then? Huh! Bad eggs for Easter?

Then, on Easter morning, when they were sitting down to breakfast at the farmhouse, their Auntie brought in a big coloured cardboard egg. And inside were two little yellow cheeping chicks, snug and warm on a bed of straw! "The mother hen hatched these specially for you two!" Auntie said. "You will be able to watch them with their mother while you are here." What a wonderful Easter surprise and how the Twins loved the chicks!

Clever mouse

A mouse's life is full of fun
From early morn till day is done.
They're free to run from here to there
Without a solitary care.
They laugh and sing and play all day.
"We are a happy lot," say they,
"Though cash enough to pay our way
Is what we lack – alackaday!
And so it was young Monty Mouse
Sat all alone inside his house
And thought: "I know how I can make
Some cash to buy our next cheese cake.
I'll write a book about us mice
And say what makes our life so nice."
So Monty wrote a splendid book
About the food that mice do cook,
Like bacon rinds and hard-boiled eggs
(Which they can balance 'tween their legs!)
And then he wrote about *the cat*,
A really fearful subject that!
But now to cut our story short
A wealthy publisher then bought
Young Monty Mouse's story which
Made him and all the mice quite rich.

The lion's roar

There was once a lion who was very proud of being the King of the Jungle. Not only was he the strongest and cleverest animal of all, he was also the noisiest. He had a roar that shook the very trees to their roots. The other animals in the jungle wished at times that that nuisance of a lion would stop roaring and allow them a little peace.

Then one bright and sunny morning when the lion opened his mouth to roar, no sound came – not even a whisper. He had lost his voice. Oh dear, was he *annoyed!*

On the other hand, there was so much peace in the jungle, the zebras, the monkeys, the elephants and the giraffes, were delighted.

Then upon a day as the lion prowled along he heard the sound of human voices. Creeping stealthily nearer, he overheard several human hunters discussing how they could capture some animals for a circus. Beside himself with rage, the mighty lion leaped into the middle of the humans' camp. Then he opened his great mouth and the lion *roared* and *roared* and *roared!*

The hunters were so surprised they leaped into trucks and drove away at top speed along the jungle track, never stopping once and looking back.

Realising he had found his voice again, the lion was very pleased with himself – but not as pleased as all the other animals when they knew they had been saved from captivity by the brave lion.

Overjoyed that they could continue to live happily in their jungle home, they all cheered the lion and told him that in future they would not mind how loud he roared. "After all, are you not the *King* of the Jungle?" they said and you saved us from the circus.

Choirboy Jim

Little Jim sang in the church choir every Sunday. One early morning on his way to church, he saw a mouth-watering red and green apple on a tree by the gate of the vicar's house.

"That's for me," chuckled hungry Jim. So jumping up, he picked the apple and scampered up the path leading to the church.

"Hurry up, little Jim," smiled the vicar. "We are all waiting for you." So Jim changed quickly, took a couple of bites of the apple and joined the other choir boys.

He hid the apple behind his back and awkwardly held his hymn book in his other hand. But the book was too heavy for little Jim to hold like that for very long.

Suddenly he dropped the apple. Clutching the hymn book with both hands, he watched the apple roll along the floor only to be stopped by the slim foot of the vicar's wife.

"Ah, Jim," she said when the service was over. "I see you like picking apples – especially the vicar's. So how would you like to pick the rest of them?" What could Jim say but "Yes"? Oh dear, it took *ages*. But when he had finished the vicar's wife said: "And now you can take as many as you like for yourself." So all ended happily for Jim.

Sammy Stork

The animals and birds had built a railway in Lakesville. It ran from Bluebell Wood to Yellow Cornfield. Sammy Stork was made Ticket Collector and he was proud of his important new job. Then one evening, when he was flying home, the strap broke on the money pouch which he wore round his neck, and the pouch and all the ticket money Sammy had collected was lost. Sammy looked everywhere for it but there was no sign of it.

"What are you looking for?" asked a tiny field vole looking up at Sammy. When Sammy told him, the little vole said he would help him and it was not long before the little vole had found the pouch. Mrs. Field Mouse was just about to use it as a nest for her babies and the ticket money was still inside, safe and sound. Sammy *was* pleased.

"I wish there was something I could do for *you*," he said.

"Well," said the vole, "perhaps while you are flying around you could look about for some corn for us. We're all very hungry and winter is on the way."

Then Sammy thought of Yellow Cornfield, and how his trains went there. So he gave the vole and mouse family special free tickets to visit it whenever they liked! And they had a wonderful time collecting enough corn for the whole winter.

Captain Bevan

The world's great seas do number seven
And lord of all is Captain Bevan.
You see him here upon the poop
Of his good ship "The Chicken Soup!"

Now pirates far and wide, 'tis told,
Were frightened of this seaman bold.
He hunted them from here to there
And sank them all – and didn't care!

When war broke out, he sailed the seas
In search of Britain's enemies,
And when he found them, just for fun,
He shot to bits full forty-one!

With no more ships to sink, the war
Was at an end and so – on shore
Came Captain Bevan to his house.
And fainted when he saw *a mouse*!

Balloons for sale

The man who sold balloons at the end of Linda's street was having a bad time. The weather was so wet and no-one was buying his lovely balloons with dolls attached. One of the dolls was sad about this. She knew the man would have no money at all if he did not sell some balloons soon. She made up her mind to help him if she possibly could.

When the man was looking the other way, the doll tugged her balloon free and away it sailed.

By chance it sailed towards Linda's window. She was in bed because she had fallen and hurt her leg. Her mother saw the balloon and, opening the window, she pulled it inside. She smiled and turned to Linda:

"Look! A doll has come to cheer you up!" her mother cried. "And that gives me an idea. I will pop down to the corner and buy the other doll balloons and we will have a party for all your friends."

And that is what she did. The little doll was very pleased that her idea had been such a success and that the balloon seller had sold so many balloons.

She enjoyed the party as much as anybody and it *did* cheer up Linda.

Sunshine Sue

Sue is one of those very lucky people for whom the sun always seems to shine. One summer term at school, Sue's teacher decided to take the whole class on a picnic. They would hire a bus and go away into the country for the whole day.

"It is lucky for us that Sue is in this class," said the teacher, "because whichever day we choose for our picnic is bound to be sunny. It's always sunny for Sue."

So the day was chosen and the children began to get very excited. Sue intended to have a word with the sun about the picnic because she knew it was important that he should know which day it was. But every day for a whole *week* before the picnic, the sun did not shine at all! It seemed that the sun had not been listening to Sue.

"You had better tell your friends to take their raincoats," said her mother the day before the picnic. "I don't think the sun is going to shine tomorrow."

Well, Sue's mother was right. It *was* a dull day when they set off in their bus. Sue *was* disappointed. But when they arrived at the picnic place, the sun appeared, and it shone all day!

The next morning, when Sue woke up, the sun was shining again, right into her bedroom window.

"There, Sue!" the sun seemed to say. "I just had to have a little joke with you—I wouldn't have let you down really!"

And Sue winked at him happily, knowing that she could still be called Sunshine Sue.

Winter Robin

What a dull and dreary time is winter when the days are so cold and the winds blow so angrily. And yet the robin seems quite happy as he hops around, his bright eyes searching for the odd berry or wriggly worm. And why is the robin always so cheery? Well, he's the fellow who is always telling funny stories to the other birds.

This is one of the robin's funny stories.

A big window said to a small window: "I feel ill."

"So do I," said the little window.

"Ah," groaned the big window, "but my panes are bigger than yours."

Paper boats

Paper boats, I love you so
On the water to and fro,
As I huff and puff and blow,
Paper boats, now off you go!

Sail away and back to me,
Mummy made you and, you see
You must do your best to float,
She won't make me another boat.

"Tom," she says, "just one more blow
"In the bath you then must go!"
So, paper boats, get ready now –
I'm just about to blow – *and how*!"

Stolen gold

Farmer Dinkle was coming home from market feeling very happy. He was carrying two bags full of gold. He had sold all his crops as well as the calves and lambs that had been born on the farm earlier in the year.

But alas, his happiness did not last long. A wicked bandit held him up, stole his money and made off with it.

"A whole year's work gone for nothing," Farmer Dinkle groaned.

But the thief could not spend two bags of gold at once. So he decided to hide it in a hole in the ground not far from Farmer Dinkle's farm.

"I'll return in three days' time and help myself to some of it," he thought. But the thief had hidden the money in a fox-hole, and that same night the angry foxes pulled it out of their hole. And next day Farmer Dinkle found it, and a sad farmer was a happy farmer once more for he had gone into town and sold his pigs for two more bags, and now he has four.

The windmill

All the day the winter winds did blow
And round the windmill's sails did go
And wearily they seemed to sigh!
I often stopped to wonder why.
I could not understand those groans
That sounded like a hundred bones
All rattling in a bucket old –
But windmills sound like that, I'm told.
Then one day as I stood to stare
At that big windmill churning there,
It seemed in whisper soft to say:
"Oh dear, I do feel tired all day.
"For whirling round and round, you see,
"Is dreary work, you must agree;
"And though I turn around a lot,
"I never wander from this spot.
"But simply stand upon this mound
"And throw my spinning arms around.
"Oh, who would choose to be a mill
"And stand stock-still upon a hill?
"If I could only have my way
"I'd – like the blubells – dance all day.
"Ah no, a windmill's lot, I fear,
"Is not a happy one, my dear."
At last I knew what those groans meant
As thoughtfully I homeward went.

A clever pig

Punky the pig loved pears and he licked his lips when he saw a big juicy pear at the very top of a tree. Well, he knew he could not reach it himself but just then, Mervin Magpie flew down. Now Mervin was very vain. "Hello, Mervin," called out Punky. "I say, you're always telling everyone how strong you are – but I don't believe what you say."

"Rubbish!" snorted Mervin angrily. "Of course I'm strong – VERY STRONG!"

"Then prove it by plucking that pear from the top of that tree," said Punky craftily. Whereupon Mervin flew up, plucked the pear and flew back to Punky with it. But Mervin was no fool. He insisted on sharing the pear with Punky, and Punky had to agree.

The three apples

It was eleven o'clock in the morning, two hours since breakfast and two hours before lunch. Kenneth, Lucy and Alice were feeling hungry so they slipped into the kitchen in search of something to eat. And what did they see? Three lovely big apples on the table.

"Aha," chuckled Kenneth. "One for you, Lucy, one for you, Alice, and one for me!"

They were just about to bite into their apples, when Mummy bustled into the kitchen. When she saw them she looked angry.

"Put down those apples at once and be off with you!" she cried angrily. Kenneth, Lucy and Alice took to their heels, still hungry and now very disappointed. But Mummy had a surprise for them. After lunch, she gave them a toffee apple each. They were the same apples they had nearly eaten.

Sandcastles

Sammy had been taken to the seaside by his Mummy and Daddy. But after three days on the beach Sammy hadn't made a friend. It seemed that all the other children had their own friends or were playing with their brothers or sisters. Poor Sammy *did* feel lonely for there was no one for him to play with.

Then on the fourth day there was a Sandcastle Competition on the beach, and Sammy gleefully set about building a really splendid castle.

"I may have no friends, but I'll win the competition," he told his mummy. "Just you wait and see!"

But Sammy didn't. A big boy kicked a huge bouncy beach ball high into the air, and it fell on Sammy's castle just as he was putting the finishing touches to it.

A little girl was building a castle next to Sammy. She felt so sorry for him as he stared at the ruins of what, a few moments before, had been a truly magnificent castle. "Help me build *my* castle," she said. They made such a grand castle together that they won first prize and what was more, Sammy had a good friend for the rest of his holiday and when they went home they wrote to each other each month.

Ride-a-cock-horse

What is Susan smiling at, smiling at, smiling at?
What is Susan smiling at?
Ah, no-one really knows.

What is Susan thinking of, thinking of, thinking of?
What is Susan thinking of?
Clad in pretty clothes.

What is Susan dreaming of, dreaming of, dreaming of?
What is Susan dreaming of?
As to and fro she goes.

Why does Susan laugh all day, laugh all day, laugh all day?
Why does Susan laugh all day?
Heedless of all woes.

She's dreaming she's a lady fair, lady fair, lady fair.
With silken hair and rings to wear
And bells upon her toes!

Saying goodbye

These jolly mice are here to say
"This book has reached its end.
We hope you've liked each little tale –
May we on that depend?

"And that perhaps you'll close this book
With a regretful sigh!
We really hope that's so because
It's time to say goodbye.

"No doubt you'll now go off to play
Or else it's time for bed!
Forgive us if we now depart
For all is done and said.

"A hundred stories and one more!
Without a doubt – *enough*!
And so farewell – we're off to play
A game of blind man's buff!"